To my mother, Betty, who always cheered me on at all my performances. Even when they were just in the backyard.
—R. W.

To Christy, the busiest cat I know
—X. Y.

FLAMINGO BOOKS
An imprint of Penguin Random House LLC, New York

First published in the United States of America by Flamingo Books, an imprint of Penguin Random House LLC, 2023

Copyright © 2023 by Reese Witherspoon

Visit us online at PenguinRandomHouse.com.

Library of Congress Cataloging-in-Publication Data is available.

Manufactured in China

ISBN 9780593525128

10 9 8 7 6 5 4 3 2 1

TOPL

Design by Sophie Erb
Text set in Poppins

BUSY BETTY
& THE CIRCUS SURPRISE

by
Reese Witherspoon

illustrated by
Xindi Yan

FLAMINGO
BOOKS

Hi!

Hello!

Howdy!

I'm Betty!

Everyone calls me Busy Betty because I wake up every day with a MILLION questions and a BILLION ideas.

Today I have the BEST idea! It's my mom's birthday, and I'm going to throw a party for her.

Shh . . . it's a surprise!

My best friends, Mae and Jeffrey, are helping me make a list of all the things my mom likes.

"We need petunias! Party hats! Purple punch! And a puppy, of course, right, Frank?" I ask.

"You're making a mess, Betty," says Bo. "Quit clowning around!"

CLOWNS?!?!

Hold on! This one time when I was little, I remember seeing a clown at the circus. They sure do wear a lot of makeup.

Sweet cinnamon biscuits—that's it! We can make a circus for my mom's birthday.

A humongous, tremendous, stupendous circus! It will be the greatest day in the history of the universe!

Jeffrey is the best juggler in the world.

**Does anyone have
an extra shoe?**

Mae was the first one in our class to do a cartwheel, and now she does them all the time!

And I watch my mom put on makeup every morning! So I'm basically a professional makeup artist.

"Wow, Betty, that color goes great with your eyes!"

"It's called cherry red, but it doesn't taste like cherries to me."

Okay, our circus makeup is perfect!

Now we just need . . .

COSTUMES!

"When your mom sees this birthday circus surprise," Jeffrey says, "she's going to FLIP!"

"That's what we need to do . . ."

FLIP!!!

We need a trapeze so we can fly high in the sky!

Whoa, whoa, whoa—I feel dizzy!

Hold on. We have
to focus to finish!

You can't have a
circus without a . . .

TENT!

"We can use this tablecloth!
I'm sure my mom won't mind.
It has stripes just like a circus tent."

I think our birthday circus surprise is almost done! We have makeup, costumes, a tent, a juggler, AND a trapeze!

Uh-oh, is that my parents' car I hear?

"Quick, what are we missing?!"

"A lion!" says Mae.

Well, we don't have a real live lion,
but we do have a real live . . .

I'll be the lion trainer! Now I just have to get Frank the Lion to roar.

"Frank, lions don't yawn, they roar!"

Oh wait! How could I forget?
Frank will never roar without a . . .

TREAT!

"Introducing Frank the Lion!"

(I wonder if my mom will even recognize him!)

Jumping juggling biscuits! My mom's birthday circus surprise is gonna be . . .

"Next month," says Bo.

"Betty, don't you know Mom's birthday is next month?"

WHAT!?!?

Busted biscuits, it's not my mom's birthday?!
Which means we made a circus for no reason.
And she's about to be here!

When she sees this, she's gonna think this is . . .

WONDERFUL!

"Oh, Betty," says Mom. "This circus is perfect! It doesn't matter that it's not *actually* my birthday."

"But what do we do with our circus now?"

"Well, Betty," says Dad, "you always have a million billion ideas. And it looks like you already have an audience!"

That's it! We'll invite the whole neighborhood to our . . .

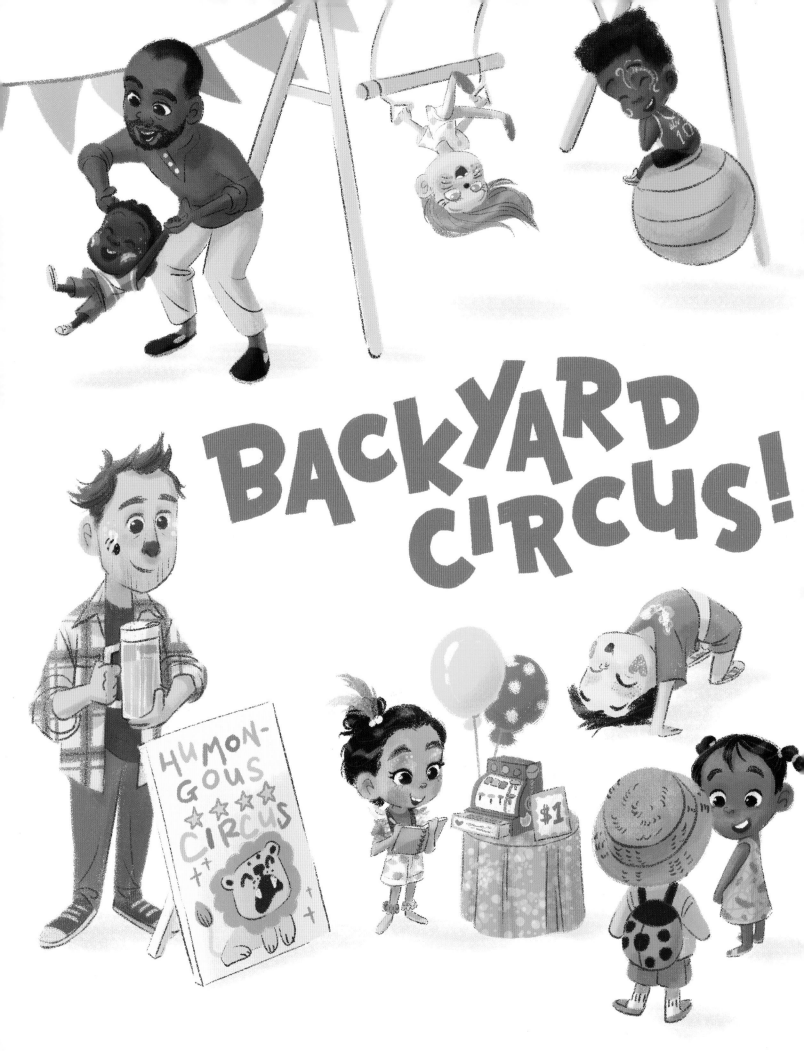

"Step right up, step right up! Welcome to the greatest show ever! Or at least the greatest show in our neighborhood!"

Sweet cinnamon biscuits, this really was the greatest day in the history of the universe!

Now, if only I could get Frank to roar.